DreamWorks

Shrek the Third

THE PHOTO NOVEL

Shrek the Third: The Photo Novel
Copyright © 2007 by DreamWorks Animation L.L.C.
Printed in the United States of America.

Library of Congress catalog card number: 2007930657
ISBN 978-0-06-122953-4
Book design by Joe Merkel
❖
First Edition

DreamWorks
SHREK THE THIRD™
THE PHOTO NOVEL

Adapted by
Amy Court Kaemon

HarperEntertainment
An Imprint of HarperCollinsPublishers

DRAGON

QUEEN LILLIAN

PRINCE CHARMING

MERLIN

Backstage...

SNIFF!

SNIFF!

SNIFF!

...Prince Charming makes a decision.

OH MOMMY!

I can't let this happen! *I* am the *rightful* king of Far Far Away!

No one will stand in my way!

The next morning, in the castle...

Good morning.

SIGH!

Good morning! Good MORNING!

ACHK!

KNOCK! KNOCK! KNOCK!

You have a very full day filling in for the king and queen.

There are several functions that require your attendance, sir.

Oh joy.

Now, let's get a move on.

In the cathedral, Shrek knights the bravest of the brave...

UMMM...

OHNO OHNO OHNO....

...or at least he tries to.

I knight thee...

ER...

SGGGU- URSH!

AAAAAHHH!

YAAAAH!

OOPS!

In the harbor, Shrek breaks a bottle of champagne over the bow of a ship...

BON VOYAGE!

...maybe a little *too* hard...

YIKES!

HELP!

HELP!

...and the ship sinks.

GASP!

Shrek and Fiona prepare for a royal ball.

Okay, you've had a tough run, but we are gonna make sure you look your best!

Raul, the castle's stylist, has his work cut out for him.

I will see what I can do.

UGH!

Shrek is pampered...

OUCH!

...and primped...

OH NO!

GRUMBLE!

GRUMBLE!

...until he looks as royal as an ogre can look.

SIGH!

Fiona and Shrek are both carefully dressed in the fanciest—and itchiest—clothes in the kingdom...

Uh, is this *really* necessary?

Quite necessary, Fiona.

I'm *SHREK*, you twit.

I don't know how much longer I can keep this up, Fiona.

I'm sorry, Shrek. It's just until Dad gets better.

Ladies and gentlemen, Princess Fiona and Sir Shrek.

As the curtain parts, Shrek gets some help with an itch...

Scratch it, Fiddlesworth!

SCRATCH! SCRATCH! SCRATCH!

? ? ? ? ?

EEEEEEEEEEWWW

In his embarrassment, Shrek stumbles and falls on a loose plank...

OOOF! OUCH!

...that sends Fiddlesworth flying high in the air!

BOING!

UM...

OH NO!

As platters of treats are brought in from the kitchen...

...Fiddlesworth falls, sending flaming skewers flying like arrows.

HOT

OOOH!

SHRIMP! MY FAVORITE

HOT

HOT!

Soon, the whole banquet hall bursts into flames.

RUN!

RUN!

AHHHHH!

19

My dear boy, you and Fiona are the next in line for the throne.

An ogre as king? There's got to be somebody else...

Anybody?

Aside from you there is only one remaining heir. His name is Arthur.

Arthur?!?

I know you'll do what's riiiiight...

KROAAAK!

OH SHREK!

SNIFF!

SNIFF!

ly the next morning...

SNIFFLE!

SNIFF!

But high above the lily pond...

...someone else is watching.

HMMM...

At night, at the Poison Apple tavern...

AHEM! What does a prince have to do to get a *drink* around here?

What do *you* want, Charming?

Just a chance at *redemption.*

And a *fuzzy navel.*

The next day, Shrek and his pals leave on their quest to find Arthur.

I will *never* forget you. You are the love of my life.

As are you...

I don't want to leave you either, baby. But Shrek is lost without me.

Shrek... maybe you should just stay and be king.

It's not that... You see...

C'mon, There's no way I could ever run a kingdom. That's why your cousin Arthur is the perfect choice.

Fiona, soon it's just gonna be you and me. I promise. I love you.

Shrek kisses Fiona and joins the others on the boat.

Back on dry land...

Worcestershire

What kind of place is this?

Well, my stomach aches and my palms are sweaty.

Must be high school.

Who rolled a "dork" spell and summoned the beast?

He's over there.

Can you tell me where I can find Arthur?

Shrek spots two students about to joust...

YAAAAAH!

WHHH!

KA-THWUMP!

The joust ends quickly, with one loser...

Ow!

And one champion.

There's no *sweeter* taste on thy tongue than *victory*.

Does Arthur look like a king or what?

36

Did you just say you were looking for Arthur?

Greetings, your Majesty. This is your lucky day!

Stop squirming, Arthur.

I am *not* Arthur.

WHAT!?!

THWUNK!

I am *Lancelot*. That dork over *there* is Arthur.

Please don't eat me.

Eat him! Eat him!

I'm not here to eat him. He's the new King of Far Far Away.

WHAT?!?

Lancelot doesn't believe it...

Artie a *king?*

More like the Mayor of *Loserville.*

41

43

Inside, Fiona and the princesses flee through a secret passageway.

Everyone in! *Now!*

The fairy-tale creatures barricade the door.

We'll hold them off as long as we can!

48

They taste the food to make sure it's not *poisoned*.

Don't worry. You'll be safe with the help of your bodyguards.

GASP!

We don't want Artie here getting the wrong idea.

UMMM...

Artie quickly runs to the ship's wheel...

Uh, Artie?

What are you *doing*?

...and tries to turn the ship around.

What does it *look* like?! I'm going *back* to school!

This isn't up to *you*!

Sorry to disappoint you, but I'm going *back*!

The ship lists and lurches...

This *isn't* getting you out of *anything*.

We're heading back to Far Far Away one way or another.

LAND HO!

...and wrecks on a beach...

On land...

...Artie stumbles on...

Mr. Merlin?

Worcestershire Academy's old magic teacher?

wha?

But before Artie can say anything else, the trio takes off into the forest...

Artie, we've got a lot of ground to cover.

...but they are a little lost.

I'll give you directions, but only after you take the journey to your soul.

53

Now look into the smoke and tell me what you see.

There's a baby bird and a father bird in a nest.

Wait, the dad just flew away...

The baby bird's trying to fly, but it doesn't know how to...

Artie suddenly remembers his own father.

Meanwhile, Fiona and the princesses make their way through Far Far Away's secret passages...

This place is *filthy*.

We're gonna find out what Charming's up to.

They emerge in the courtyard, and Rapunzel takes off.

Come *on*, this way!

60

Moments later, they are at the border of Far Far Away.

WHOA!

But when Puss opens his mouth, Donkey's voice comes out...

I've been abracadabra'd into a Fancy-Feasting, second-rate *sidekick*.

And when Donkey speaks...

At least you don't look like some bloated roadside *piñata*!

I'm really sorry, guys.

Don't be! You got us back, kid.

The kingdom of Far Far Away.

Shrek surprises Charming in his dressing room...

Break a leg.

Or, on second thought, let me *break it for you.*

Charming spots Artie...

This is supposed to be the new King of Far Far Away?

That's *enough*, Charming. I'm here now. You got what you wanted. This isn't about him.

Shrek confesses to Artie...

You weren't really next in line for the throne. I was. Okay?

You were *playing* me the whole time.

As Artie storms away, Shrek is captured by Charming and his henchmen.

I have your badge number, Tin Can—

...the princesses get two new inmates.

Donkey?

Where's Shrek?

Charming's got him. And he plans on killing Shrek tonight in front of the whole kingdom.

GRRRRRRRr!

RRRRIPP!

Do we want our happily-ever-after or not?

And together, they storm the gates...

HUH?

HEY!

C'MON!

Fiona and the princesses hurry inside...

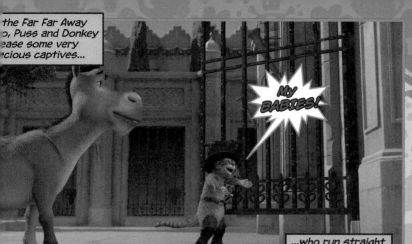

...na and the princesses make their / through the castle courtyard...

DORIS!!!

...nd Doris distracts the guards.

HI, BOYS!

As the guards race toward them, Sleeping Beauty does her thing...

HEY!

OOF!

ZZZ! ZZZ!

With the guards taken care of, Fiona and the princesses have nothing standing in their way...

Outside the castle gates, a defeated Artie heads out of Far Far Away...

Artie!

Where's the fire, señor?

You both *knew* what was going on the whole time.

He was *using* me.

Shrek only said those things to *protect* you.

Charming was going to kill you. Shrek saved *your* life.

That night, everyone gathers for Prince Charming's much anticipated show...

I wait alone up here. Locked up—please set me free.

'Tis I! Princess, my love, at last you shall be freed.

I'm strong and brave and dashing. With soft and bouncy hair.

You are about to enter a world of pain with which you are not familiar...

And torches Charming's sword...

WHA?!?

GASP!

GASP!

Suddenly, Fiona and all the fairy-tale creatures take the stage...

SAUSAGE ROLL!

GRRRRRRR!

Gingy yanks Rapunzel's extensions off her head...

HUH?

AAAH!

And Puss and Donkey rush the stage...

Pray for mercy from...

Donkey and *Puss!*

Like a born hero, Artie leaps onto the stage...

Who really thinks we should end things this way?

WHAT?

You want to be *villains* your whole lives?

84

But we *are* villains. It's the only thing we know how to do.

Did you ever want to be something *else*?

You morons!

ATTACK THEM!

But the villains stay where they are...

It's hard to come by honest work when the whole world's against you.

It's true.

mmmff?

85

Just because people *treat* you like a villain, doesn't mean you *are* one.

The thing that matters *most* is what *you* think of *yourself*.

Artie's words get through to the villains and they drop their weapons...

KLATTER!

KA-KLANK!

It's yours if you want it.

Back in Shrek and Fiona's swamp...

GA GA

Ah, *Finally.*

93